Mickey's Young Readers Library • Mickey's Young Readers Library • Mickey's
Mickey's Young Readers Library • Mickey's Young Reade
Readers Library • Mickey's Young Readers Library • Mickey's Young Readers Library
Readers Library • Mickey's Young

This Book Belongs to:

Mickey's
Young Readers Library

VOLUME
7
Donald's Dream

© MCMXC **The Walt Disney Company.**

Developed by The Walt Disney Company in conjunction with Nancy Hall, Inc.

Story by Justine Korman/Activities by Thoburn Educational Enterprises, Inc.

This book may not be reproduced or transmitted in any form or by any means.

ISBN 1-885222-40-8

Advance Publishers Inc., P.O. Box 2607, Winter Park, FL. 32790

Printed in the United States of America

0987654321

Donald woke up one bright, sunny morning. "Today is a good day to go fishing," he thought. "I'll go and borrow Grandma Duck's fishing pole. And I can dig for worms in her garden."

So off he went to Grandma Duck's farm to tell her about his fishing trip. But she shook her head and pointed to her bare vegetable garden.

"What about your promise to help me plant my garden?" Grandma asked. "If we don't get the seeds planted soon, the vegetables won't have time to grow."

Donald looked at Grandma Duck's bare garden. "It's a lot of work to dig and rake and plant and water," he thought.

"I'd love to help you," Donald fibbed. "But I need my overalls to work in the garden, and they have a hole in them. I meant to mend them, but I didn't get around to it."

"Listen to me, Donald," Grandma scolded.
"Never put off till tomorrow what you can do
today."

Donald promised to go home and mend his
overalls right away. Then he would come back to
help Grandma plant her garden.

When Donald came home, he couldn't find any thread.

"I know," he thought. "I'll go and ask Daisy for some thread."

So off he went to Daisy's house. When Donald got there, Daisy was glad to see him—at first!

"If you keep your promise to patch the hole in my roof, I'll mend your overalls for you." Daisy said.

Donald looked up and moaned. "It's a lot of work to patch a hole way up there," he said.

"But, Donald, you've promised to fix it so many times now ..." Daisy replied. "You've been putting it off for months! Every time it rains, water goes through that hole into my kitchen."

Donald agreed to patch the roof right away. But when he took out Daisy's ladder, he remembered he had broken two steps on the ladder the last time he used it. He had been meaning to fix the ladder, too.

"I can't patch the roof until I fix this ladder,"
Donald told Daisy. "But I promise to do that right
away. Today! I'll be back soon," Donald told her.
Then he took the ladder home to fix.

Donald was determined to fix the ladder, patch
Daisy's roof, and plant Grandma's garden—that is,
until he got back home.

Donald went to his garage to look for his hammer and nails. What a mess he found! Donald had been meaning to clean out the garage. But he kept putting it off, because it's a lot of work to clean a garage.

"Hammer and nails. They must be here somewhere."

But Donald couldn't find them. He got so mad, he kicked a box. Books spilled out. Now the mess was even bigger than before!

"How can I fix the ladder without my tools?"
Donald grumbled. Then he suddenly remembered.
He'd left his hammer and nails at Scrooge's house.
So Donald set out for Scrooge's.
On his way, Donald passed Goofy's house.
"Gee, maybe Goofy has a hammer and some
nails I can borrow. That way I won't have to go all
the way to Uncle Scrooge's house."

"Gawrsh, Donald. I don't have any hammer
and nails," Goofy said. Then he added, "I sure am
glad you came by, though. Maybe you can help me
fix my bike. It's hard to deliver newspapers without it."

"Okay," Donald sighed. "But to fix your bike I'll
need Mickey's wrench. I'll be right back."

As he walked, Donald was getting tired just
thinking about all his chores.

Donald was so busy thinking of all he had to do that he stepped right into one of Pluto's holes.

"What's going on?" Donald asked in surprise.

Mickey sighed, "Pluto thought my wrench was a bone, and he hid it somewhere in the garden."

"I wanted to borrow your wrench to fix Goofy's bike," Donald moaned. "You'll help me find the wrench, won't you fella?" Donald asked Pluto.

But Pluto pretended not to hear Donald.
"I guess Pluto is angry at you," Mickey
explained. "You never brought those bones you
promised him."
"But, I don't have the money to buy dog bones.
Uncle Scrooge hasn't paid me yet," Donald said,
"because I never finished my work for him."

That's when Donald remembered about the hammer and nails at Scrooge's house. As he said good-bye to Mickey, he once again promised Pluto that he would bring him some bones—soon! Then Donald rushed to Scrooge's house to get the hammer and nails so he could fix the ladder, patch Daisy's roof, and plant Grandma's vegetable garden.

When Donald arrived, Scrooge scolded him for not finishing his work.

"By the time you get around to putting in that new alarm, someone will rob my money bin!" Scrooge shouted.

Donald felt badly when Scrooge scolded him.
But putting in that alarm system was very hard work.
"I'll be back to do it soon," Donald promised,
taking his tools.

Scrooge shook his head. "When is soon?" he
called after Donald. "Twenty years from now?"

Donald went straight to the garage with his
hammer and nails. He really was going to do all the
things he had promised. He would fix the ladder
and patch Daisy's roof. He would put in Scrooge's
alarm, buy those bones for Pluto, fix Goofy's bike,
and plant Grandma's garden.

But first he had to clear off his worktable. It was
then that he saw one of the books that had fallen
out of its box. Donald picked it up and started to
read. He forgot all about his work and his promises.

Donald started to read. But he was so tired from his very busy morning that before he got very far in the story, he fell fast asleep.

While Donald was dreaming, he heard the
sound of footsteps. He looked around. Everything in
the garage looked old and dusty. Then Donald saw
someone he thought he knew. He was wearing a
suit of rags and an old top hat. It looked like . . .
could it be . . . his Uncle Scrooge?

"How long have I been sleeping? And what's
wrong with Uncle Scrooge?" Donald wondered.

Donald stared at the old duck standing before him.

"What happened?" Donald asked.

"I was robbed," Uncle Scrooge told him sadly. "They took all my money, because I had no alarm."

"Oh, no!" Donald groaned.

Then Donald remembered the other promises he had put off. What had happened to his other friends during his long sleep? Donald walked down the streets of his town, looking for his friends.

"There's Pluto!" Donald cried, as he looked unhappily at the thin, hungry-looking dog.

"I never did bring that poor dog those bones I promised," Donald said sadly.

The sound of a newspaper hitting the sidewalk made him turn. Before him stood a very old and tired Goofy, carrying a giant sack of newspapers on his back.

Donald sighed. "I never did help Goofy fix his bike so he could deliver his papers."

"What about Daisy?" Donald thought. He ran as fast as he could to her house.

"Row, row, row your boat," the once-pretty duck sang sadly. She rowed around the small lake that had formed around her house.

"If only I had patched the hole in her roof,"
Donald thought. "I'm so sorry, Daisy," Donald said.
"It's too late now," Daisy replied, looking sadly
after her goldfish as it swam past her in the lake.

"Too late!" Donald exclaimed, suddenly remembering Grandma Duck's garden. Donald raced to Grandma's farm.

He walked past the garden. It was covered with weeds. Donald peeked through Grandma's kitchen window. There he saw her boiling bare bones in a small pot of water. She was trying to make soup.

"Donald Duck!" Grandma said with surprise. "Where have you been all this time?"

She set a place for him at the table. Then she poured some watery soup into his bowl.

"Oh, no—it's all my fault!" moaned Donald. "If only I had listened to you, Grandma. You told me not to put things off. I was planning to listen. I just kept putting it off!"

Donald tossed and turned in his sleep. One arm bumped into the worktable, knocking it over.

"Huh?" Donald woke. When he sat up, the open book fell to the floor. Donald looked all around the messy garage. Nothing was old and dusty after all.

"It was just a dream!" he said happily. "And it isn't too late to do everything I've been putting off."

He fixed the ladder and took it over to Daisy's.
Before she could say, "Hi Donald," he was up on
the roof, patching the hole. Then he thanked Daisy
for mending his overalls, and he hurried off to put in
Scrooge's alarm.

Scrooge watched in surprise as Donald worked.

"I didn't know you had it in you, my boy," Scrooge said gladly as he paid Donald for a job well done.

Donald didn't have time to wait around for more praise. He rushed off to buy Pluto some bones, get the wrench, and fix Goofy's bicycle. Then he raced over to Grandma's farm.

Donald started to dig the dirt in Grandma's garden. Grandma smiled as she watched. She could hardly believe her ears when Donald told her all the things he had done that day.

"You know, it really *is* better to get things done than it is to put them off," Donald said.

When the garden was all planted, Grandma
thanked Donald for his help. Then she added, "Now
it's time for you to do something else you've been
putting off. And Grandma handed Donald a picnic
basket full of wonderful food, and a fishing pole.
   "Remember, dear, don't put off till tomorrow
what you can do today! Have a good fishing trip!"
   And Donald did just that.

Think About It

Dream-A-Story

Point to the picture of the characters in the order in which Donald saw them *while he was dreaming*. (If you need help remembering, look back at the story.)

After your child does the activities in this book, refer to the *Young Readers Guide* for the answers to these activities and for additional games, activities, and ideas.

Donald's Doings

After Donald has his dream, he gets busy keeping his promises. Look at each picture of Donald. Tell what he is doing and for whom.

1.

2.

3.

4.

5.

6.

Fix-It Word Search

In the word search below, find the six tool words listed on Donald's tool box. (Hint: Words may be found from top to bottom and left to right. The same letter may appear in more than one word.)

W	R	E	N	C	H	L
N	A	S	Q	H	C	A
A	K	H	Y	A	T	D
I	E	O	M	M	G	D
L	A	V	O	M	X	E
S	H	O	V	E	L	R
L	C	Q	D	R	R	Y

SHOVEL   HAMMER

NAILS   RAKE

WRENCH   LADDER

Tool Jumble

See how many of the tool word labels below you can unscramble. (Hint: Look at the words in the tool box on page 44 to help you.)

SLAIN

HRENWC

DDREAL

MMRAHE

HOVELS

KREA

ckey's Young Readers Library • Mickey's Young Readers Library • Mickey's Yo
ung Readers Library • Mickey's Young Readers Library • Mickey's Young Read
Mickey's Young Readers Library • Mick